The Simple Giant

Other brilliant stories to collect:

The Simple Giant

Retold by
Alan Temperley

Illustrated by
Mark Edwards

SCHOLASTIC
Home of the Story

Scholastic Children's Books,
Commonwealth House, 1–19 New Oxford Street,
London WC1A 1NU, UK
a division of Scholastic Ltd
London ~ New York ~ Toronto ~ Sydney ~ Auckland
Mexico City ~ New Delhi ~ Hong Kong

First published by Scholastic Ltd, 1999

ISBN 0 590 13498 1

Printed by Cox and Wyman Ltd, Reading, Berks.

2 4 6 8 10 9 7 5 3 1

Once upon a time, in a Scottish village, there was a big boy, and a kind sea captain, and a lazy farmer, and an old woman with a cat. This is their story.

The good ship *Sark* was far out at sea. For two days she had been battling

a storm. The white sails were furled. Waves crashed across the deck.

At midday a cry came from the lookout, high in the crow's nest.

"Boat ahoy! Two points to starboard!"

Captain Angus, who had not left the bridge for a day and a half, put the telescope to his eye. All he could see were tumbling waves. For an instant something dark appeared – then was gone.

"Starboard wheel," Captain Angus ordered the helmsman.

Ten minutes later the object

revealed itself as a rowing boat, full to the brim but still afloat. There was somebody in it – a young boy. He was waving.

Captain Angus brought the *Sark* alongside and a sailor went down with a line. He fastened it round the boy's chest and he was heaved aboard. The brave sailor followed and the next minute the rowing boat was lost

behind them in the waves.

One of the crew took the boy by the hand and led him from the stormy deck into their cabin. The sailors gazed at him in surprise. He had blue eyes and appeared about five, but he had the build of a sturdy boy twice that age.

Captain Angus descended from the bridge. "What's your name, son?" he asked gently.

"John," the young boy said and gave a sweet smile.

"He's simple in the head," murmured one of the sailors.

"And where do you come from?" said Captain Angus. "What were you doing in that rowboat?"

"John," he said again, eager to please.

And no one ever discovered, even after he had learned to talk, where the boy had come from, or what he was doing adrift in the storm.

The sailors were kind. They gave him a good meal, a warm hammock with blankets, and fresh clothes. And several days later the *Sark*, with billowing sails and flags flying, was sailing up the silver Solway and winding river to her port in the south of Scotland.

When she was spotted, like a great white swan between the fields of

barley, families and villagers hurried down to the quay. The ship was moored. Sailors hugged their wives and children. Captain Angus descended the gangway, closely followed by young John.

"Who's that?" exclaimed the villagers, for the boy was frightened by their staring faces and kept opening and closing his mouth like a fish. "Ahhh!" he said, hiding his eyes, and clutched the captain's jacket.

"We picked him up at sea," said Captain Angus. "In the storm."

"Send him back," cried the

superstitious villagers. "Look at him, he's not right. He'll bring bad luck." They crossed themselves. "Put him in a boat before it's too late and let the sea take him."

"Nonsense!" said Captain Angus. "He's not strong in the head, that's all. He's shy. You've frightened him." He put an arm round the big boy's shoulders. "You're coming home with

me, aren't you, John."

"Mmm! Unh!" said John with tears in his eyes.

"My wife and I will decide what's best for him."

The following day Captain Angus and his wife, who had no children of their own, announced that they were adopting the boy.

And so John became their son.

But when his new mother went to throw out the ragged clothes he had been wearing in the rowing boat, she found a piece of paper in the pocket of

his jacket. In smudged ink she read:

His name is
John Boe

And because, after his clothes had gone, this was his only possession, that is what they called him.

For seven years John lived with Captain Angus and his wife in their pretty cottage above the shore. His parents loved him and he was very happy. Slowly he learned to understand what they were saying and to talk in a simple fashion. Three years

after his arrival, when he was eight, as his mother guessed, he was sent to the village school.

The teacher despaired. He had never taught a pupil like big John Boe. When kind words and sweets and patience failed to drive a little learning into the boy's head, he tried threats and punishment. But all his anger and whacks on the seat of the

boy's trousers produced no better result. Instead John, who could have lifted the teacher and set him on top of the cupboard had he wished, gave his sweet smile and pointed to the sunlit window. "Look," he said. "Birdies make nest." Then he returned to his tiny desk and lowered his head above the mysterious numbers.

In the end, through his teacher's and his mother's efforts, John did learn a little reading and writing, and the most simple of counts.

Yet although his schooling was slow, how John grew! By the time he

went to school he was as tall as his father. And at twelve he was inches taller than the biggest man in the village. He had a thatch of light brown hair, his shoulders were broad and his boots had to be specially made.

But when he was twelve a terrible thing happened. Captain Angus was drowned at sea; his wife pined away

and died shortly afterwards; and the captain's dishonest brother claimed the house and all their money.

What was to become of the heart-broken boy? What was to be done with him? The villagers held a meeting.

"You can't expect *me* to keep him," said a neighbour. "A great lump like that! He'd eat me out of house and home."

"Why should the parish pay for him?" said the minister. "He's not one of us."

"He came from the sea, didn't he?" said a third person. "Let him live in a cave and eat seaweed."

Not everyone was so unkind, but nobody was willing to give the boy a home.

The children who had been John's classmates pushed him round and round and chanted:

"Daftie John! Daftie John!
   Put him to work
   And give him a scone."

And in the end this is what happened. A fat and lazy farmer named Gowrie, whose crops were never gathered in time, whose buildings were tumbling from neglect, and whose animals starved in the fields, realized how much work he might get out of such a strong, simple-minded boy, and how little he would have to pay him. As if it were a great kindness, he offered to employ John as his odd-job man.

So John Boe said goodbye to his big warm bed, and the cottage where he had been so happy, and moved

into a corner of a leaky barn, on a muddy farm, to work for a bad master who always carried a whip or a stick as he went about the fields, and when he saw that John did not retaliate, he used them frequently.

For seven years John laboured for Farmer Gowrie. His fields were hedged and ditched; the buildings were made sound and watertight; the cattle in the pasture were fat and content; the crops were hoed; the grain was reaped and dried and stored in the barn. And for all this

work John received not one shilling of wages, not even the children's scone; nothing but bread and water, a dish of oatmeal in the evenings, and whatever leaves and berries he could find in the hedgerows.

Despite this he continued to grow, and by the age of nineteen, when another change took place in his fortunes, he was a man more than seven

feet tall, and so strong that when a cart went off the road or a cow went into a ditch, he could lift it back to safety.

One summer afternoon, as John was walking through the village on an errand, he came upon a gang of children tormenting a cat that they had driven into a corner.

"Stop that!" John boomed.

"Look, it's John the daftie!" shouted one of the boys, and threw a stone which bounced off John's leather waistcoat. "Go on back to the asylum! It's Lucky Maxwell's cat. She's a witch

and we're going to kill it." He pulled
a rock out of the ground.

"Stop it!" John cried again and
ran at them, his arms waving and big
feet slapping the ground. Clods of
earth rattled about his head, sticks
struck him on the back. Shielding
himself, John hurried through the
gang and picked up the terrified cat,
nursing it against his chest. "You're

bad children!" he said. "Lucky Maxwell's a nice old lady. Puss never hurt you. Leave it alone."

Deprived of their victim, the children turned on John. Words flew like missiles.

"Cuckoo!" they shouted. "Stupid donkey!"

"My dad says you should be locked up."

"Can't spell cat,
    C-A-T,
    Chop off his head
    And send him to sea!"

John was used to their taunts.

Head bowed to protect the animal in his arms, he walked away and soon reached the tumbledown cottage of Lucky Maxwell.

"Oh, my poor little Blackie!" said the bent old woman and took the cat from him.

"They were going to hurt it," John said. "They're *bad* boys and girls."

"I know, they're very cruel sometimes." She stroked the cat's ears. "But you're kind. Come in, if you can get into my little house."

Feeling honoured, for people never invited him into their homes, John

bent almost double and squeezed through the doorway. In the living-room he had to sit on the floor because none of the chairs was big enough or strong enough for him. Beams ran overhead and the leaded window looked out on an overgrown garden.

It was a strange house. An owl blinked down from a crowded dresser

and hooted softly at the young giant
who filled half the room. A family of
hedgehogs rustled in a box of straw.
Bunches of herbs hung drying. Books
and bottles and pieces of apparatus
stood on the dusty ledges.

"I've just been baking," said the
old lady. "Would you like a slice of
warm bread with raspberry jam?"

"Yes, thank you," said John politely.

He had not enjoyed such a treat since his mother died.

But one piece looked very small in his big hand, so Lucky cut a second slice. It was delicious. In the end John ate the whole loaf and nearly finished the jam as well.

Then it was time to go. Already John was late and would be in trouble. Carefully he rose, trying not to upset a table or knock over ornaments.

"You're a good young man," said Lucky Maxwell. "I've seen how the villagers and that brute of a farmer treat you. Tell me, if you could have

anything in the whole wide world, what would you like most?"

John was confused. People never asked him questions like that. After a lot of thought and hard breathing he said, "I'd like to be brave – and famous."

"Why?" she said.

"So people won't tease me any more."

"Indeed yes." Now it was Lucky's turn to think hard. "And why not?" she said at length. "Get a name as a good worker and you can lie in your bed all day."

"Indeed yes," said John, who liked the sound of the words.

"Get a reputation as a rich man and you can live your life in rags."

John nodded vigorously. He had no idea what she was talking about.

"Here." The old lady crossed to a shelf and lifted down a pot of honey. "If you want to be brave and famous, do exactly what I tell you. Tomorrow

midday, when the sun is high and hot, carry this pot of honey past the gallows on the highroad. Do you understand?"

John concentrated. "Yes," he said, and reverently took the jar from her hand. "Tomorrow dinner time ... when the sun's hot ... past the gallows."

"Take the top off first," she said.

"Take the top off," John repeated.

"Good." Lucky Maxwell smiled. "Don't forget. And thank you for bringing Blackie home."

"She's a nice puss." John bent to go through the doorway. "I like her."

When John said he wanted the day off work – his first day in seven years – Farmer Gowrie was furious. "Day off work? Are you mad? Where did you get that idea? Who's going to milk the cows? Who's going to cut the barley, hoe the turnips, stack the hay, clean out the pig sty? Do you expect me to do it? The answer's no! It's not convenient, not convenient at all."

But all his anger, and threats, and blows on John's broad back, could not make the young giant swerve from his determination.

And so, the following midday, when the sun was at its highest and heat made the distance dance, John walked along the winding highroad past the empty gallows. He had washed at the farmyard pump that morning and put on his best clothes and bonnet. Puffs of dust at every step turned his boots and ankles white. Perspiration made the shirt stick

to his back. And worst of all, the
smell of the honey attracted flies
from the hillsides all around. In a
maddening cloud they buzzed
around his head, and landed on his
sweating face, and settled in the
jar. He broke off a frond of bracken
and waved it to keep the flies away.

After a mile he halted and looked
around. The road was empty. Not even
birdsong disturbed the baking
countryside. John was puzzled. He
thought: Lucky Maxwell had not
said in which *direction* he was to walk.
Perhaps he had gone the wrong way.

Anxiously John trotted and walked and ran back to the gallows. The noose hung motionless. He continued for another mile and halted again. The road remained empty; nothing moved on the shimmering hillsides.

The sweat ran from his hair. He loosened his shirt.

Very disappointed, he sat down
at the side of the road and set the
honey pot between his knees.
Perhaps Lucky Maxwell had been
teasing him like all the others!

The flies were thicker than ever.
His vision was filled with their
dancing bodies. Their buzzing
filled the air. He struck at them
with his bonnet. A scatter of dead
flies landed in the honey and
bowled across the white dust of
the road. There were a lot. With a
twig John began to pick them from
the jar.

"One – two – three –" he counted, but he kept losing track. He raked them from the road towards his boots and started again. "One – two – three –" but again he lost count and he was never very good beyond ten anyway. But there were a *lot*. In the end he settled for a hundred. A hundred seemed an enormous number. And out of the blue – for no reason he

was aware of – a little rhyme jumped
into his head:

Here am I, great John Boe,
Who killed a hundred at one blow.

The words delighted him and he
said them several times. Then he
thought he should write them down
because otherwise he was bound to
forget. From a little tin of treasures in
his pocket he took a stub of charcoal.
But what could he write on? A
bleached tree stump stood on the hill-
side. He broke off a flake of wood and

returned to his seat. Brow wrinkled with concentration, he wrote:

HEAR AM I GRAT JOHN BOE
WHO KILED 100 AT WON BLOE

It took a long time to get it right. When he had finished he read it over and smiled happily. He was a poet! Then, his reason for being on the highroad half forgotten, and worn out with the unaccustomed mental exercise, he lay back on the heathery bank and fell fast asleep in the sunshine.

A while later, as John was gently snoring, a gang of ragged soldiers came marching along the road. They were not dressed in uniform, but working smocks and britches, and for weapons they carried spades and scythes and dung forks. They were not regular soldiers but a hastily-assembled body of farm labourers, brought together by a bold Scottish laird named Sir

Donald McGregor. Their intention was to fight and repel a force of English redcoats who were raiding north of the Border, looting and killing wherever they went.

When they saw the sleeping giant, Sir Donald ordered his men to halt. Who could he be? One of the soldiers spotted John's rhyme written on the sun-bleached wood. Swatting back the flies, he read it aloud to the others:

"Here am I, great John Boe,
Who killed a hundred at one blow."
Sir Donald looked at John's

tremendous arms and shoulders. "A hundred at one blow, eh?" he said. "This young fellow should come with us. What do the rest of you think?"

"Aye!" they cried aloud. "Hurray!"

And before John knew what was happening, they had woken him from his sleep, set him astride a big Clydesdale stallion, and he was being carried along the road in their midst.

"John Boe, eh?" said Sir Donald. "And where do you come from?"

"Tell us about the men you killed," said one of the soldiers.

"What did you use for a weapon?" asked another, thinking of Samson. "The jawbone of an ass?"

John was frightened and totally bewildered. Who were these armed men? What were they talking about? Where were they taking him? He tried to speak but no words would come, just panting and gasps and gulps.

Soon they came to the gallows, standing high and black at the side of the

road. John flung his arms around the post to stop them taking him any further. The soldiers urged the Clydesdale forward. John would not let go. With a loud SNAP the gallows broke off at the bottom. John rode on, the big gallows clutched across his chest.

"Aye," exclaimed the men around him. "That's a grand weapon for a warrior like you."

They stole a tin of paint and pulled a sheet from a farmwife's washing line. One of the soldiers wrote John's rhyme across it in big red letters and they held

it aloft like a banner.

> HERE AM I,
> GREAT JOHN BOE,
> WHO KILLED 100
> AT ONE BLOW!

Fresh volunteers, attracted by the hero in their midst, left their work and ran to join the force. Wives and children watched from the doorways.

In the late afternoon, as the high-road descended from the hills to a broad plain, the Scots — some bare-foot, some armed with no more than a

stick — came face to face with the English troops, all in battle array, with scarlet jackets and weapons gleaming in the sun. The Scots were outnumbered.

They halted. Two hundred metres apart the opposing armies faced each other across the heather and boggy ground. Sir Donald thrust John to the front of his ragged band.

"Go on," he hissed.

John eyed the ranks of English with their fine clothes and long sharp spears.

"Go on!" Sir Donald urged impatiently.

John looked at him, wild-eyed with alarm, and backed away.

Sir Donald was furious. "Go on, you great gowk!" He grabbed the horse's reins and dragged him back. "Tell them who you are!"

John was terrified. Dimly he realized that something was expected of him — but what? From the corner of his eye he spotted his banner waved aloft.

Some of the Scots were pointing at it. Desperate to placate Sir Donald, who was even fiercer than Farmer Gowrie, and hoping this was what he wanted, John roared aloud:

"HERE AM I,
   GREAT JOHN BOE,
   WHO KILLED A HUNDRED
   AT ONE BLOW!"

At the same moment one of the Scots jabbed a dagger into the Clydesdale's rump. With a wild whinny it leaped forward and galloped headlong across the plain towards the English ranks. It was a magnificent horse; its hooves splashed, its tail flew. John clung to its mane with one hand, screaming "Aaahhh! Aaahhh!" with fright at the top of his voice. In his other hand the gallows flailed like some terrible weapon of destruction.

The English stared in horror, then as one man they turned tail and fled

in disarray.

At John's back the Scots gave a roar of triumph and charged in pursuit.

The victory was total. The English were routed. Many were captured and imprisoned, the rest driven back south of the Border.

John was a hero! His horse was recaptured, and as the Scots returned home he rode at Sir Donald's side at

the head of the column. The red and
white banner fluttered overhead, and
as they passed through villages,
crowds came flocking to cheer the
great warrior, news of whose exploits
had gone ahead.

John loved the attention, although
he had no idea what he had done to
deserve it, and did not like to ask in
case it suddenly ceased. To the end of
his life he never quite understood.

When they reached home there
was a feast in his honour. Everyone
was invited. Sir Donald sat on John's
right side, and Lucky Maxwell, with

Blackie in her lap, on his left. Farmer Gowrie made a speech in which he proclaimed how he had been preparing John for this glorious day; Captain Angus's dishonest brother declared how he had always looked on John as one of the family; the children who had stoned and taunted him, wanted to touch the great man; no one suggested that he should be sent back to sea. And in the midst of the celebrations, head and shoulders above the rest, John smiled happily and held out his plate for another helping.

As for Sir Donald, he refused to be parted from his hero and set John up as keeper in the turreted gate-house of his estate. John's rhyme was chiselled in stone above the entrance, enough in itself, without sight of the bold warrior, to keep burglars and poachers from Sir Donald's land.

The following year John met and married a little milkmaid, who was proud of her famous husband and looked after him. They had many friends, and in time seven children – big strong boys and pretty girls. And there in that house with its high rooms, with fields and woods spread all around, and the river winding to the silver sea, they all lived happily ever after.

Other stories to collect:

Aesop's Fables

Malorie Blackman
Illustrated by Patrice Aggs

Once upon a time there was a man named Aesop
who told stories full of wisdom...

Hansel and Gretel

Henrietta Branford
Illustrated by Lesley Harker

Once upon a time there were a brother and sister
who were left alone in the forest...

The Snow Queen

Berlie Doherty
Illustrated by Siân Bailey

Once upon a time there was a little boy whose
heart was turned to ice...

The Twelve
Dancing Princesses

Anne Fine
Illustrated by Debi Gliori

Once upon a time there were twelve princesses,
and no one knew why their shoes were full
of holes...

Grey Wolf, Prince Jack and the Firebird

Alan Garner
Illustrated by James Mayhew

Once upon a time there was a prince who set out
to seek the mysterious firebird...

Mossycoat

Philip Pullman
Illustrated by Peter Bailey

Once upon a time there was a beautiful girl whose
mother made her a magical, mossy coat...

The Six Swan Brothers

Adèle Geras
Illustrated by Ian Beck

Once upon a time there was a brave princess
who saw her six brothers turned into swans...

The Three Heads in the Well

Susan Gates
Illustrated by Sue Heap

Once upon a time there were two stepsisters —
one good, one bad — who both went out to seek
their fortunes...

Cockadoodle-doo, Mr Sultana!

Michael Morpurgo

Illustrated by Michael Foreman

Once upon a time there was a rich and greedy sultan who met a clever little cockerel…

Rapunzel

Jacqueline Wilson

Illustrated by Nick Sharratt

Once upon a time there was a baby who was stolen by a witch…

Rumpelstiltskin

Kit Wright

Illustrated by Ted Dewan

Once upon a time there was a beautiful girl who
would die if she couldn't spin straw into gold…

The Goose Girl

Gillian Cross

Illustrated by Jason Cockcroft

Once upon a time there was a princess who lost
everything she had ever owned…